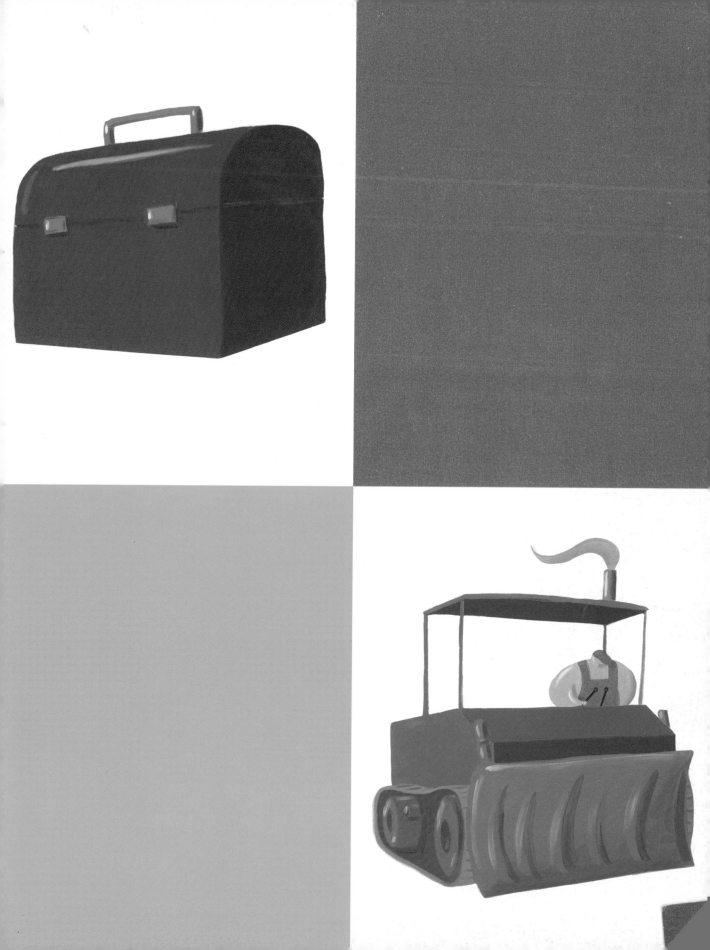

bill
martin
books

Bill Martin Jr, Ph.D., has devoted his life to the education of young children. Bill Martin Books reflect his philosophy: that children's imaginations are opened up through the play of language, the imagery of illustration, and the permanent joy of reading books.

Henry Holt and Company, Inc., *Publishers since 1866*
115 West 18th Street, New York, New York 10011
Henry Holt is a registered trademark of
Henry Holt and Company, Inc.
Text copyright © 1966 by Eve Merriam, © 1994 by Dee Michel
and Guy Michel. Illustrations copyright © 1995 by Dan Yaccarino.
All rights reserved. Published in Canada by Fitzhenry & Whiteside Ltd.,
195 Allstate Parkway, Markham, Ontario L3R 4T8.
Library of Congress Cataloging-in-Publication Data
Merriam, Eve. Bam, bam, bam / by Eve Merriam; illustrated by
Dan Yaccarino. "A Bill Martin book." Summary: In this noisy
poem, a wrecking ball demolishes old houses and stores to make
way for a skyscraper. 1. Wrecking—Juvenile poetry.
2. Children's poetry, American. [1. Wrecking—Poetry.
2. American poetry.] I. Yaccarino, Dan, ill. II. Title.
PS3525.E639B25 1995 811.54—dc20 94-20300

ISBN 0-8050-5796-X
1 3 5 7 9 10 8 6 4 2

First published in hardcover in 1995 by Henry Holt and Company, Inc.
First Owlet paperback edition, 1998

Printed in the United States of America on acid-free paper.∞

The artist used alkyds on bristol paper to create the illustrations for this book.

A Bill Martin Book
Henry Holt and Company
New York

BAM
BAM
BAM

Written by
Eve Merriam

illustrated by
Dan Yaccarino

Workmen are covered with white dust like snow.

Oh, come see the great demolition show!

BAM, BAM, BAM,

It's raining bricks and wood

in my neighborhood.

Down go the houses,

down go the stores,

CRASH goes a chimney,

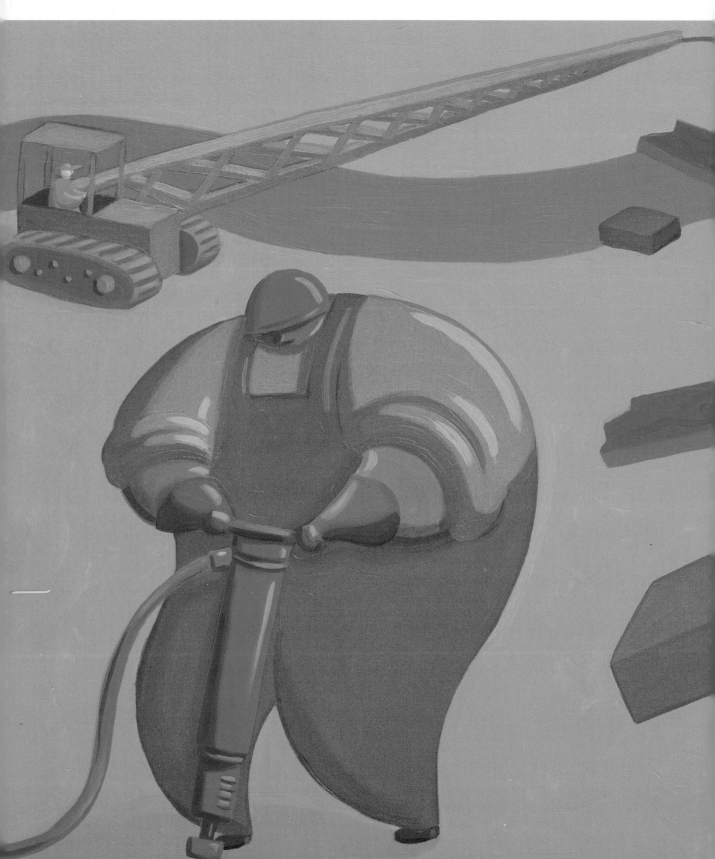

POW goes a hall,

ZOWIE goes a doorway,

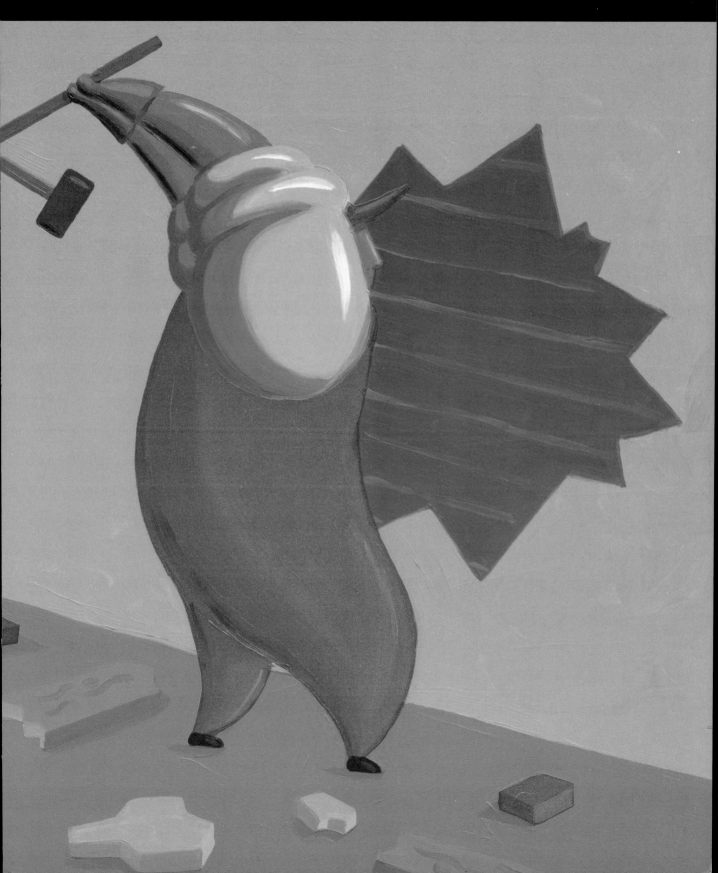

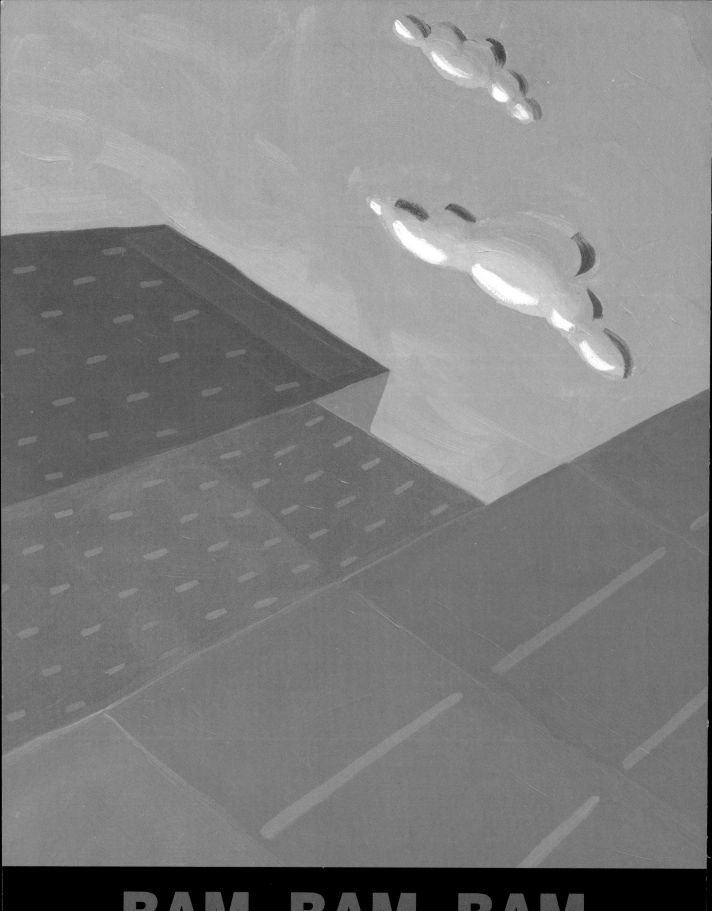

BAM, BAM, BAM,

changing it all.